Happy Trails
Barbara Knight

Wink Burgess

The RESCUE

The first story in the
"Penny the Mustang Pony"
series

by Barbara Knight

Illustrated by Dale "Wink" Burgess
in watercolor

This book is dedicated to all my friends
and family who had the faith in my dream
and helped make it a reality.

Published by MUSTANG BKS   ISBN 978-0-9766270-0-0

Third Publishing 2011

Penny awoke quickly to a clear, bright day.
She had a feeling of excitement.
She couldn't explain what it was,
but she felt as if something
was about to happen.

Penny got her name from her Mother because
of the color of her shiny coat. It sparkled like a brand new
penny when the sun shined on it.
    Penny didn't like being the youngest pony in the
herd. She'd see the older ponies out in the meadow running
and frolicking. She often had dreams of playing with them.

"Penny, Penny" Star cried. "Get up, hurry, and come see what I found!"

Penny couldn't believe these older ponies, Pickles and Star, wanted to play with her. Penny didn't move right away, which caused Pickles to snort and shake her head.

"What's the matter don't you want to go play?" teased Pickles. "Come on, we're wasting a beautiful day."

"Mother, can I go play with Pickles and Star?" Penny asked. Sassy, her Mother answered, "Yes, you can go play, but stay out of trouble."

Penny and the two ponies ran off with their manes and tails flying.

As they ran by, Ben, another young pony in the herd yelled, "Can my friend Jako and I come play with you?"

"Sure, we're going exploring," answered Star.

All the ponies galloped away for another day of adventure. The rest of the herd was soon out of sight as the friends ran down an old dry creek bed.

Suddenly Star stopped running and cried out, "There it is, come look!"

Penny stood with her friends trying to see what Star was so excited about.

Then Penny saw it! There was a cave in the side of the hill. Ben got excited and said, "Let's go in and explore."

The ponies looked at one another and then at Penny. "No way," Penny said. She remembered what her Mother had said about staying out of trouble.

That cave looked like trouble!

"What's the matter Penny, are you afraid to go into the cave?" teased Pickles.

Penny turned to leave but Pickles galloped off to the cave. Soon the others followed her.

"No Pickles, please don't go in there," cried Penny. She spoke too late.

Her four friends had entered the darkness of the cave.

"What could it hurt? No one will know," thought Penny as she started to follow her friends. Penny slowed to a walk as she remembered her Mothers words.

Suddenly the ground began to rumble, and with a deafening roar, a big cloud of dust billowed out of the cave. Penny cried out to her friends, but the only response was the sound of the rocks settling as the dust cleared. Her friends were trapped in the cave!

Instantly Penny turned around and ran as fast as her sturdy little legs could carry her back up the dry creek bed. Within minutes she was sprinting across the open meadow to her parents and the rest of the herd.

Penny's Father, Apache, saw Penny running toward them.
Sassy stopped grazing and lifted her head as she heard Penny's cries.

"Mother, Father, come quick! My friends are trapped in a cave!"
Penny was breathless, so she could hardly tell them what had happened! Apache told the other mothers and fathers what had happened. The herd was off like a stampede toward the cave!

Penny's little heart was pounding! It was hard to keep up with the herd, but fear for her friends gave her strength to catch up with Apache. She knew her friends were trapped behind the rocks at the entrance of the cave.

Apache saw the problem at once and motioned for the other horses to use their hooves to pull away the rocks.

Within moments they were helping. They dug furiously at the small rocks until they reached a large boulder that had broken from the top of the cave and blocked the entrance. Apache and the other horses leaned into the large boulder with their shoulders, and giving a furious shove, they were able to push it aside.

The faces of each of her friends told the story of fear and pain. Jako had a cut on his nose. Dust covered Star's coat.
A bump had risen in the center of Pickles forehead. Ben came limping toward them.

Penny could see a twinkle in her friend Star's eyes and knew her friends would be okay.

Apache scolded them all for their foolishness. "You could all have been trapped forever, if Penny had followed you into that cave."

Sheepishly, the young ponies hung their heads in shame. Each promised to be more careful and stay closer to the herd.

Penny

Ben

Pickles

Star

Jako

All the ponies gathered around Penny, who had
shown wisdom by refusing to enter the cave. She had been
able to run for help to save them. Soon the near tragedy was
forgotten.

The ponies raced around the herd as they all
made their way back to the meadow, with Penny in the lead.

MUSTANGS

In the mid 1800's mustangs were used in many ways. The Spanish people who came here to settle left the pony roaming on the North American Continent.

As more people migrated West to homestead, they saw these wild horses and used them to build their own herds.

The Cavalry and the Indians also caught them to use. The Pony Express liked them because they were very durable and sturdy.

Quiz

1. How did Penny show courage and wisdom?

2. How did Penny save her friends?

3. Name two things you can do to be like Penny.

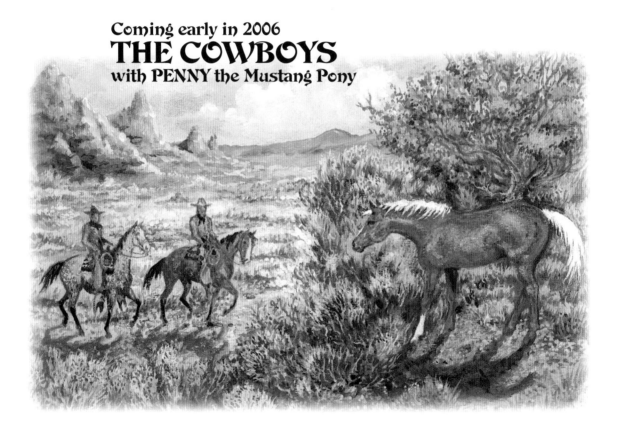

Coming early in 2006
THE COWBOYS
with PENNY the Mustang Pony

For more information or ordering books contact:
Barbara Knight at
MUSTANG BKS - P.O. Box 1193 - Crooked River Ranch, OR 97760
or visit our web site at www.mustangbks.com
or call: 541-504-9620
e-mail: bknightmustangbks@netzero.net